This igloo book belongs to:

...Rian Ross..♡

Contents

igloobooks

Published in 2016
by Igloo Books Ltd, Cottage Farm, Sywell, NN6 0BJ
www.igloobooks.com

Copyright © 2016 Igloo Books Ltd

Illustrated by Maxine Lee
Written by Melanie Joyce

Designed by Justine Ablett
Edited by Jenny Cox

LEO002 0616
2 4 6 8 10 9 7 5 3 1
ISBN 978-1-78557-631-7

Printed and manufactured in China

Farm Stories

igloobooks

Cock-a-Doodle-Oink!

Cockerel woke the animals early one day on Merry Dale Farm.

Cock-a-Doodle-Doo!

"We've got to get ready for the Big Farm Show tomorrow,"

he said.

So, everyone got busy **washing** and **brushing** and **polishing**.

All except Duckling, Piglet and Calf, who ran around playing chase.

Oink-oink went Piglet, **slipping** and **skidding**. He **splattered** mud on Dog and **tumbled** into Calf, who **crashed** into Duckling who **knocked** over the water bucket.

Cock-a-Doodle-Doo!

"Behave yourselves. Otherwise you won't go to the show,"

said Cockerel.

Duckling, Piglet and Calf **didn't** listen to Cockerel.
All day long, they chased each other **round** and **round**.
By the afternoon, everyone was fed up with them.

"**stop messing about!**"

cried Cockerel, just as Piglet **knocked** over a
milk urn, which got **stuck** on Cow's foot.

Cow **bellowed** and **frightened** Duck...

... who **flapped** and **panicked** the mice...
... who **squeaked** and **spooked** Horse...

... who **neighed** and **startled** Pig...
... who **squealed** and **scared** Cat.

There was complete chaos on Merry Dale Farm.

COCK-A-DOODLE-DOO!

went Cockerel, as **loudly** as he could.

"Off to bed with you three!"

said Cockerel, puffing up his feathers in the most alarming way.

Duckling, Piglet and Calf **slunk** off to bed, realizing that they should have done as they were told.

"We won't be allowed to go to the show now,"

said Calf.

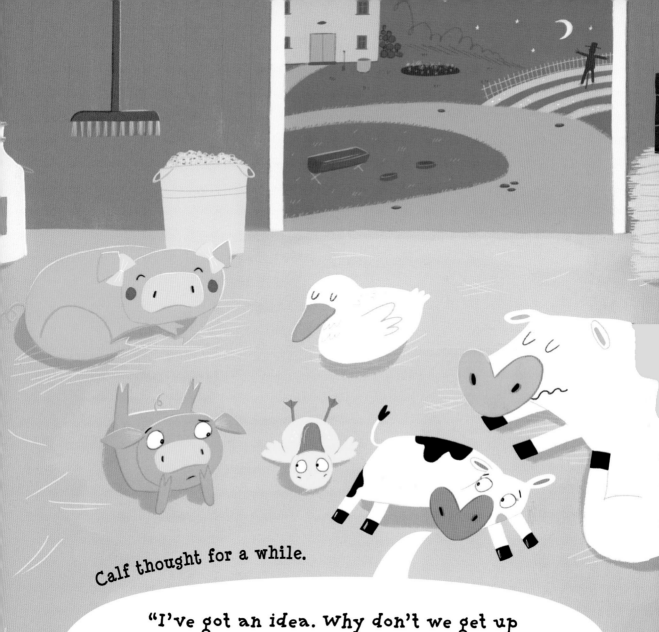

Calf thought for a while.

"I've got an idea. Why don't we get up early tomorrow morning and be extra quiet? Everyone will see we can behave ourselves, then we will be allowed to go to the Big Farm Show!"

he said.

Early next morning, Duckling, Piglet and Calf crept
across the farmyard, but all they could hear was
snoring and **snorting**.

"They're still asleep,"

whispered Duckling.

Then they saw Cockerel strutting around with his beak
wide open, but with **no sound** coming out!

"He's lost his voice!" said Piglet.

"It must have been all that shouting yesterday," said Calf.

"We'll have to wake everyone up. All together now, one... two... three..." said Duckling.

QUACK-A-OINK-OINK-MOO!

Suddenly, everyone woke up.
"You've saved the day!" said
Horse, as she quickly got ready.
"Come on, there's just enough
time to get to the show."

"Well done, Duckling,
Piglet and Calf.
You can come to the
show, after all,"

whispered Cockerel
in a croaky voice.

Everyone had a **super** time at the Big Farm Show, especially Duckling, Piglet and Calf. Just for once, they were allowed to make as much **noise** as they liked... and they **loved** it!

QUACK-A-OINK-OINK-MOO!

Little Chick's Big Adventure

One day, Little Chick and Mother Hen went to the meadow where Horse was grazing near the wood.

"What's the wood like?"

asked Little Chick.

"The wood is scary,"

said Horse.

"Never go there by yourself,"

said Mother Hen.

But this just made Little Chick all the more **curious.**

14

Mother Hen and Little Chick **pecked** and **scratched** until Mother Hen settled down to roost. Just beyond the fence, Little Chick could see the wood.

As his mother fell asleep, he took one tiny step towards it. Nothing bad happened, so he took another.

In the wood, there were little streams and pretty flowers where bunnies **hopped** and squirrels **scampered**.

Little Chick played chase with the bunnies...

... and hide-and-seek with the squirrels.

The wood isn't **scary** at all, thought Little Chick.

All afternoon, Little Chick
played with the woodland
animals until it was time
for them to go home.

"Goodbye,"

he called.

"Goodbye, Little Chick,"

they said.

Suddenly Little Chick felt sleepy. He snuggled
down for a nap in the warm afternoon sun.

HOO-HOO! came a noise. Little Chick opened his eyes. The sun had gone and the sunny paths were crossed with **shadows.** Little Chick didn't know which way to go. He began to feel **cold.** He began to **shiver.**

HOO-HOO!
Owl swooped down.

"Are you lost?"

she asked.

"Yes," whispered Little Chick as he looked into Owl's big eyes.

"I can show you the way home," she said, swivelling her head.

"Let me show you," said another voice.

Fox stepped out from the shadows. He **grinned** at Little Chick, showing his **sharp**, shiny teeth.

As Fox and Owl came closer, Little Chick felt very afraid.

"Mummy was right. The wood is scary and I should have listened to her,"

he thought.

Just then, there was a **stomping** and **squawking** sound...

... It was Horse and Mother Hen! "Thank you, Owl and Fox,"
said Horse, politely. "We will take Little Chick home."

Mother Hen cuddled Little Chick close.
"Don't ever go off without me again," she said.
"I won't," said Little Chick, as he thanked Mother Hen
and Horse. Little Chick had learned a big lesson.

The Goat Detectives

chomp, chomp, **Chomp** went Daisy the goat, eating Farmer Bill's prize roses, one morning.

"Mmmm, these are absolutely yummy,"

she said.

"Try the red ones, Daisy. They're positively delicious!"

said Myrtle.

Just then, Farmer Bill came out of the barn. His face went a sort of purply red, just like a **beetroot**, and he seemed in a very **bad** mood.

"Mrs Bill has put me on a diet. Yet here you two are, eating everything in sight. You can go on a diet too,"

he said, grumpily.

Myrtle and Daisy didn't like their diet one little bit. It was nothing but lettuce leaves and carrots all week long.

By Sunday morning, their tummies were **rumbling** and **gurgling** so much, they hardly noticed the terrible **commotion** coming from the henhouse.

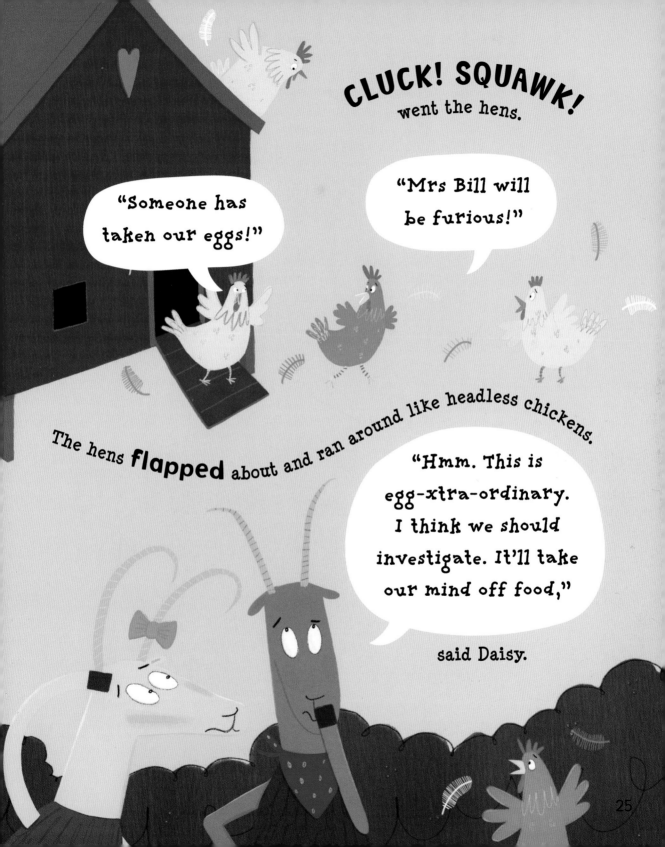

CLUCK! SQUAWK!
went the hens.

"Someone has taken our eggs!"

"Mrs Bill will be furious!"

The hens **flapped** about and ran around like headless chickens.

"Hmm. This is egg-xtra-ordinary. I think we should investigate. It'll take our mind off food,"

said Daisy.

25

That night, Myrtle and Daisy
crept into the farmyard.

"Look,
footprints!"

said Myrtle.

They followed the trail and it led to the henhouse,
where they saw a shadowy figure putting eggs into a sack.

There was a soft **clumping** and a
creaking as the shadowy figure crept away.

"Let's follow the thief,"

whispered Myrtle
creeping along behind.

The footprints led to
the farmhouse door.
Very carefully, Daisy and
Myrtle opened it and guess
who they found?

27

Farmer Bill!

"I was so hungry. I just wanted a few eggs. Anything but lettuce and carrots,"

he said.

Everyone felt sorry for Farmer Bill. Mrs Bill promised
he could stop dieting if he did more exercise.
So Farmer Bill promised the goats nice food if
they stopped **munching** his roses.

Daisy and Myrtle agreed and Farmer Bill gave them **delicious** things to eat. The hens got their eggs back, and Farmer Bill went jogging every day.

At last, **everyone** was happy on Red Rose Farm.

29

You Can't Do It Donkey

When the post arrived at Little Farm one morning,
it caused quite a stir.

"There's going to
be a talent competition
at the town hall
on Saturday,"

cried Goose.

The animals **whooped**, **cheered** and **chattered**
excitedly, then rushed off to rehearse their acts.

Donkey heard all the **hullabaloo** and came to see what it was about. In the sty, the pigs were practising their act.

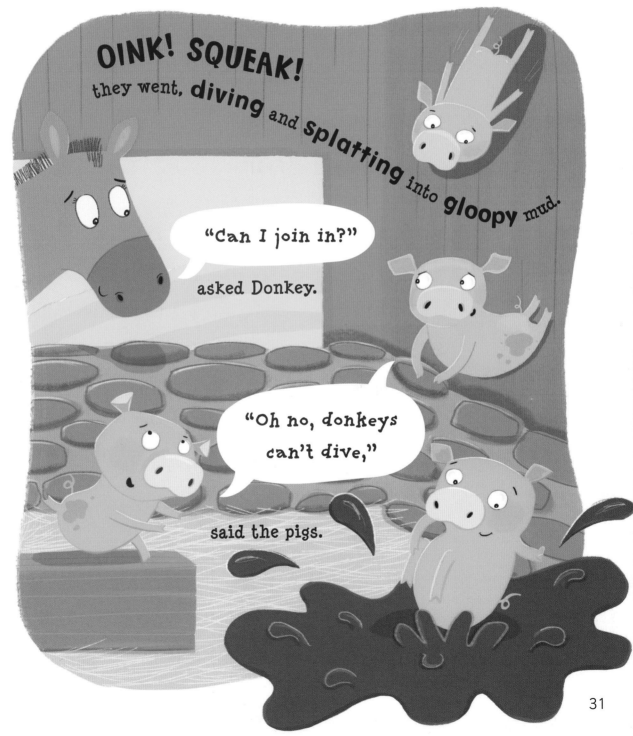

OINK! SQUEAK!
they went, **diving** and **splatting** into **gloopy** mud.

"Can I join in?"

asked Donkey.

"Oh no, donkeys can't dive,"

said the pigs.

31

So, Donkey visited the cows.
MOO, MOO! they went, **swishing** their
tails and **twirling** like great big ballerinas.

"Can I join in?"

asked Donkey.

"Oh no, donkeys
don't dance,"

replied the cows.

So, Donkey went to see the sheep.

On the farmhouse steps,
Goose was tap-dancing.

HONK! HONK!

Donkey didn't even bother
asking if he could join in.
"Everyone thinks I'm just a
stupid donkey," he thought.
"Well, I'll show them."
He trotted off to the barn and
closed the doors firmly shut.

Soon, there were some very peculiar noises coming from the barn. **Thumps** and **twangs** and **sploshing** sounds. It was all very strange.

BANG!

OUCH!

BUMP!

WHOOSH!

OOMPH!

HEE-HAW!

"Donkey is so silly!"

"It's a good job he's not in the talent show tomorrow,"

said the other farm animals, laughing.

35

The next day at the talent show, all the animals performed
their acts. At the very end, a late entry was announced.
"It's the... er, rather unusual, Donkey,"
announced the compère. Donkey trotted onto the stage...

... and pretended to be the animals on Little Farm.

The pigs... HEE-OINK!

The cows... HAW-MOO!

The sheep... HEE-BAA!

And lastly, Goose... HEE-HONK!

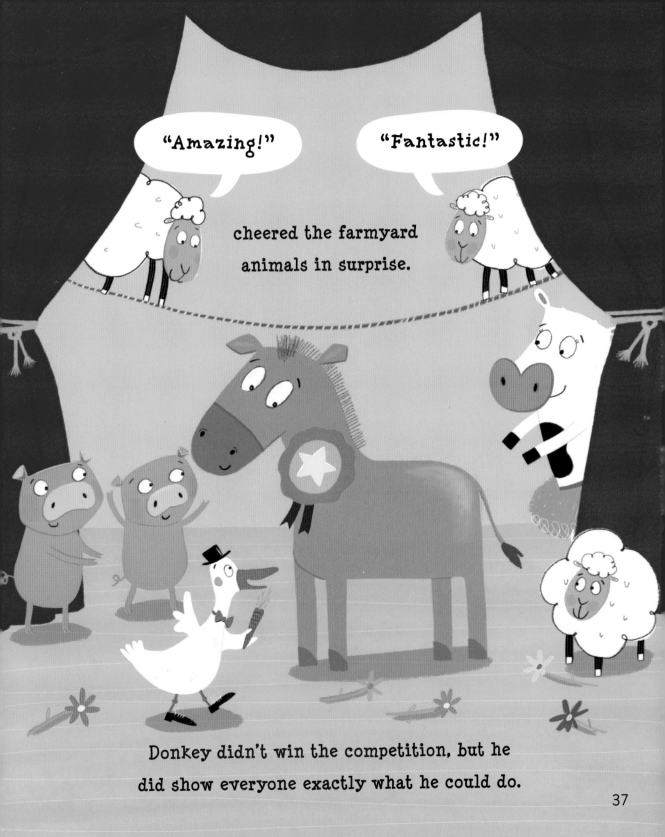

Donkey didn't win the competition, but he
did show everyone exactly what he could do.

The Great Escape

Farmer Claire was doing her best to cheer up the animals on
Willow Tree Farm, but it wasn't working. Rodney the horse was
tired of his stable, Millicent the cow kept complaining about
the cowshed and Lulu the sheep was sick of her pen.
"Nice food, warm beds. It's not such a bad life, is it?"
asked Farmer Claire. No one answered, so she sloped off.

"What we need is change. What we need is adventure!"

said Rodney.

Everyone agreed, but they weren't sure what sort of adventure.

Then, very early the next day, something **amazing** happened. A travelling circus drove right by Willow Tree Farm.

"That's it! We'll run off and join the circus,"

cried Rodney, snorting.

That's exactly what they did. They packed some snacks and snuck off when Farmer Claire wasn't looking.

Lulu was going to be a trapeze artist, Rodney was going to be a show horse and Millicent was going to be an acrobat.

They were quite sure that it just meant **swinging** on a few ropes, a bit of **cantering** around and **bouncing** on a trampoline or two. Life in the circus was going to be easy! But the animals of Willow Tree Farm were in for a nasty surprise...

Ding-a-ling! went the alarm clock at dawn the next day.

"Time to practise!"

cried the ringmaster.

Rodney cantered round and round until he felt **dizzy**. Millicent kept **falling** off the trampoline and Lulu was **afraid** of heights. All day long they practised and each night they performed in the show. By the end of the week, the animals of Willow Tree Farm were exhausted.

"You all need to work harder. Make sure tonight's show is a really good one!"

said the ringmaster.

"I miss Farmer Claire,"

said Rodney.

"Me too,"

said Millicent.

"Me three,"

added Lulu.

They all decided that they were thoroughly **miserable** with life in the circus.

That night, the crowd **roared** and **cheered**. Then the lights dimmed. Rodney did his usual cantering around and Millicent tried to stay on the trampoline. Then, the ringmaster announced the grande finale. Lulu had just begun to swing on the trapeze when she spotted Farmer Claire sitting in the front row of the audience.

Lulu took one hoof off the trapeze, went flying through the air and suddenly lost her grip.

Oomph! She fell down, onto the trampoline.

Boing! Millicent bounced high into the rafters.

46

Bang! Millicent landed on Rodney's back and gave him such a fright, he **bolted** round the ring after the ringmaster. Farmer Claire and the crowd fell about laughing. The ringmaster, however, wasn't quite so happy.

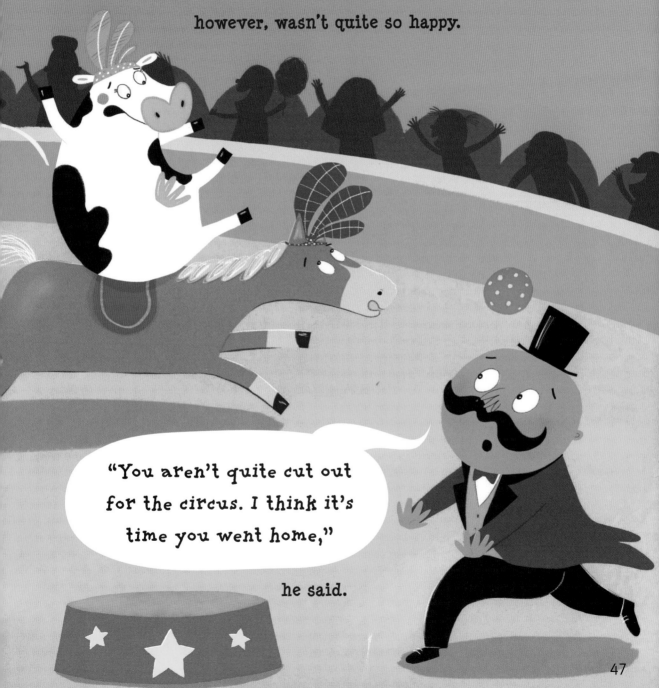

"You aren't quite cut out for the circus. I think it's time you went home,"

he said.

The animals agreed and before they knew it, they were back on Willow Tree Farm. Rodney trotted and cantered around, Millicent happily chewed grass and Lulu lazed in the sun.

"Welcome home," said Farmer Claire, with a grin.

She suspected there would be no more adventures for quite some time.